Would you rather?

Halloween Edition

Burt Lloyd

Burt Lloyd is a lover of humor and comedy in all forms. He began his career as an actor and tutored English to children as a side job. As he continued both endeavors, he combined children's education with entertainment and made it his newfound passion.

Would you rather

pick a bone off a skeleton
Or
tear a ghost off a sheet?

Would you rather

spend a night in a graveyard
Or
a morning in detention?

Would you rather
Trick
Or
treat?

Would you rather
cuddle one python
Or
put your hand in a tank of
tarantulas?

Would you rather
be haunted
Or
have to haunt a house yourself?

Would you rather
be chased by 5 slow zombies
Or
one super fast one?

Would you rather

decorate one enormous
pumpkin
Or
10 teeny ones?

Would you rather

bust ghosts
Or
fight witches?

3

Would you rather

have a zombie
Or
a vampire nibble your ear?

Would you rather

stay up all Halloween
Or
stay in?

Would you rather

take your mom
Or
your younger sibling trick or
treating?

Would you rather

wear a witches hat
Or
a mummy's bandages?

Would you rather

cross a vampire
Or
a black cat's path?

Would you rather

meet your gym teacher
Or
your math tutor trick or treating?

5

Would you rather
run from zombies with a fast friend
Or
trip them up?

Would you rather
watch kids cartoons
Or
a horror movie?

Would you rather
hide in a library
Or
a cemetery?

Would you rather
swim in blood
Or
shower in zombie drool?

Would you rather

get boogers
Or
broccoli as a treat?

Would you rather

have bloodshot eyes
Or
tombstone teeth?

Would you rather
fight zombies
Or
help them find people?

Would you rather
be cursed
Or
hypnotized by a witch?

Would you rather
ride with the headless horseman
Or
in a haunted car?

Would you rather
your costume had a hole in the
butt
Or
your candy bucket?

Would you rather

eat all your Halloween candy
Or
give it to the unpopular kid?

Would you rather

eat a giant pumpkin
Or
give up half your candy?

Would you rather
have fun on Halloween
Or
fun sized candy?

Would you rather
wear your Halloween costume all
year
Or
not at all?

Would you rather
be allowed no tricks
Or
no treats?

Would you rather
rap with a mummy
Or
howl with a werewolf?

Would you rather

be a witch
Or
a princess tonight?

Would you rather

have cobwebs in your hair
Or
slime on your pants?

Would you rather
Dracula
Or
a zombie give you a haircut?

Would you rather
have Christmas
Or
Halloween?

Would you rather
get caught stealing all the candy
Or
get away with none?

Would you rather
be a popular skeleton
Or
a terrifying ghost?

Would you rather

turn into a werewolf
once a month
Or
once a day?

Would you rather

have the hiccups
Or
indigestion on Halloween?

13

Would you rather
fall off of a witches broom
Or
into an open grave?

Would you rather
have to have a witches broom
Or
a mummy's bandages all Halloween?

Would you rather
have candy you're allergic to
Or
no candy at all?

Would you rather
be kidnapped by aliens
Or
a witch?

Would you rather

eat your family
Or
veggies?

Would you rather

be rescued from ghouls by
Captain Marvel
Or
Batman?

Would you rather
see 12 clowns at the circus
Or
one clown at a graveyard?

Would you rather
sit on a cake
Or
have a pie thrown in your face?

Would you rather
talk to a zombie
Or
sing with a werewolf?

Would you rather
hide behind the couch
Or
under the bed?

Would you rather

get money
Or
candy?

Would you rather

get bitten by a vampire
Or
kissed by a zombie?

Would you rather
speak a snake's language
Or
understand birds?

Would you rather
sleep in a crypt
Or
a mummy's casket?

Would you rather
eat broccoli
Or
some creepy pasta?

Would you rather
see fireworks
Or
a starry night?

Would you rather

dunk an apple
Or
carve up a pumpkin?

Would you rather

be cursed silent
Or
only be able to yodel?

Would you rather
a Werewolf ate your big toe
Or
all of your candy?

Would you rather
be eaten by
Or
have to eat dinner with a cannibal?

Would you rather
have detention with a math
teacher
Or
be haunted by the ghost of one?

Would you rather
watch a horror film in the cinema
alone
Or
in a noisy crowd?

Would you rather

hear a black cat meow
Or
a wolf howl?

Would you rather

Halloween decorate the
school
Or
the teachers do it?

Would you rather
be cool
Or
a ghoul?

Would you rather
be a nasty nurse
Or
a devilish costume as a costume?

Would you rather
dress up as a horrible history teacher
Or
an evil English teacher?

Would you rather
wear Dracula's cape
Or
a witches hat?

Would you rather

give the headless horseman
a hat
Or
Dracula a toothbrush?

Would you rather

wear a cool costume
Or
a warm one?

Would you rather
wear a sheet as a ghost
Or
make a bed?

Would you rather
be invisible
Or
look horrifying?

Would you rather
get given a little candy
Or
steal a lot?

Would you rather
see a demon
Or
a dentist?

Would you rather

have one candy bar
Or
a bucket of candy corn?

Would you rather

get stuck in a marsh
Or
a marshmallow?

Would you rather
get your teeth stuck together by
candy
Or
fall out?

Would you rather
have a homemade
Or
store bought costume?

Would you rather
carve a jack o lantern
Or
have the headless horseman give
you a haircut?

Would you rather
be a vampire's dentist
Or
bandage a mummy?

Would you rather

have a candy carrot
Or
a candy apple?

Would you rather

face the creature under
your bed
Or
the one in the closet?

Would you rather
have Xmas presents
Or
Halloween candy?

Would you rather
not have candy for a week
Or
eat nothing but candy for a year?

Would you rather
have no Halloween
Or
have it last all year?

Would you rather
give
Or
take candy?

Would you rather

date a vampire
Or
a werewolf?

Would you rather

find a surprise candy
Or
an old favourite?

Would you rather
be a cat
Or
a mouse for Halloween?

Would you rather
be haunted
Or
taunted by a ghost?

Would you rather
have to eat all your Halloween
candy in an evening
Or
one piece a day?

Would you rather
kiss a witch
Or
be cursed by one?

Would you rather
one pumpkin
Or
a 1000 jelly beans?

Would you rather
Trick
Or
treat at the zoo or the graveyard?

Would you rather
a zombie ate your brains
Or
your feet?

Would you rather
call Mystery Inc.
Or
the Ghostbusters?

Would you rather
dress up as an Avenger
Or
one of the Justice League?

Would you rather
get brain freeze
Or
the heebiegeebies?

Would you rather

bob for apples
Or
eyeballs?

Would you rather

have goose bumps
Or
your skin crawl?

33

Would you rather
have your nose
Or
ears stolen?

Would you rather
haunt your best friend
Or
your worst enemy?

Would you rather
have a half empty candy bucket
Or
steal your friends full ones?

Would you rather
howl at the moon
Or
sing for your supper?

Would you rather

use a skull
Or
a severed head for a candy
bucket?

Would you rather

get candy from a scary
house
Or
none from a nice one?

Would you rather
walk a lot and get lots of candy,
Or
a little and get less?

Would you rather
dance to an evil violin
Or
sing into a cursed microphone?

Would you rather
face Maleficent
Or
the Wicked Witch of the West?

Would you rather
have your palm read
Or
look into a crystal ball?

Would you rather

eat a bucket of beans
Or
one cooked eyeball?

Would you rather

have a magic book
Or
staff?

Would you rather
get an Annabelle
Or
a Chucky doll?

Would you rather
meet a creepy puppet
Or
ventriloquist's dummy?

Would you rather
lose your voice completely
Or
only be able to sing?

Would you rather
be stalked by ten tabby cats
Or
one black one?

Would you rather

be a fat clown
Or
a slender man?

Would you rather

fight a vampire with a steak
Or
a carrot?

Would you rather
be a werebunny
Or
a werehamster?

Would you rather
lose your soul
Or
your candy?

Would you rather
make s'mores
Or
just have the chocolate?

Would you rather
have fireworks
Or
a bonfire?

Would you rather

wrestle an octopus
Or
strangle a snake?

Would you rather

run the kissing booth
Or
bob for apples all night?

41

Would you rather
find false teeth
Or
a used plaster in your candy
bucket?

Would you rather
eat raw squid
Or
boiled boogers?

Would you rather
hide from one dinosaur
Or
a hundred zombies?

Would you rather
fall off of a witches broom
Or
a giant bat?

Would you rather

dig a grave
Or
fill one in?

Would you rather

there was a monster under
Or
in your bed?

43

Would you rather
wear an awesome costume
Or
a warm one?

Would you rather
wear the Red Ballet shoes
Or
Dorothy's red shoes?

Would you rather
do gravestone rubbings at midnight
Or
photograph ghosts?

Would you rather
drink 2 litres of soda
Or
water if you weren't allowed
to burp?

44

Would you rather

eat a pie
Or
throw one?

Would you rather

drink mystery soda
Or
hot apple cider?

Would you rather
get a love
Or
an invisibility potion from a witch?

Would you rather
read the Walking Dead
Or
have a Running Nose?

Would you rather
eat cabbage
Or
fight a man eating plant?

Would you rather
spend Halloween in detention
Or
a haunted house?

46

Would you rather

eat all of your candy
Or
not brush your teeth?

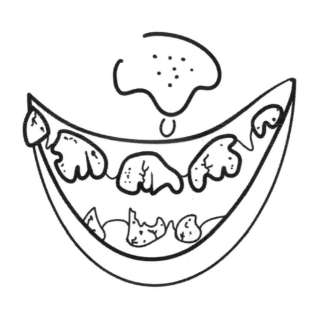

Would you rather

go on holiday to Transylvania
Or
Salem?

47

Would you rather
take out a dead frog's eye
Or
pickle a newt?

Would you rather
be able to hypnotise a teacher
Or
throw your voice?

Would you rather
be cursed to sing
Or
dance to every hit song you hear?

Would you rather
be able to see what'll happen
tomorrow
Or
last year?

Would you rather

kiss a frog
Or
a witch?

Would you rather

have 3 nipples
Or
12 toes?

Would you rather
fall into a pool of Nutella
Or
pbj?

Would you rather
be president for a day
Or
rich for life?

Would you rather
be tickled by a skeleton
Or
hugged by a slime monster?

Would you rather
live the same great day over and over,
Or
have an ordinary life?

Would you rather

eat an apple from a toilet
Or
sift candy from a kitty litter
tray?

Would you rather

have a flying carpet
Or
a flying broom?

Would you rather
take Deadpool
Or
Loki trick or treating?

Would you rather
face the zombie
Or
android apocalypse?

Would you rather
have no access to the internet
Or
have your internet history public?

Would you rather
wrestle an octopus
Or
gorilla?

Would you rather
be dive bombed by a bat
Or
a crow?

Would you rather

take brilliant selfies but actually
be ugly
Or
take an okay selfie and be
beautiful?

Would you rather

be followed by a magpie
Or
a black cat?

Would you rather

take your kid brother trick
Or
treating if you got more candy?

54

Would you rather

take your dog trick
Or
treating if he got all the candy and
you didn't?

Would you rather

spend five nights with Freddy
Or
one night with Slenderman?

Would you rather

be able to tell scary ghost stories
Or
happy, funny ones?

55